pickerel frog

northern
saw-whet owl

white-tailed
deer

white-breasted
nuthatch

purple finch

black-capped
chickadee

LOOKING
FOR LOONS

Written by Jennifer Lloyd

Illustrated by Kirsti Anne Wakelin

Library and Archives Canada Cataloguing in Publication.   Lloyd, Jennifer   Looking for loons / Jennifer Lloyd ; Kirsti Wakelin, illustrator.   ISBN 978-1-894965-54-5   I. Wakelin, Kirsti Anne II. Title.   PS8623.L69L66 2007   jC813'.6   C2007-901453-4   Book Design by Steedman Design.   10 9 8 7 6 5 4 3 2 1   Printed in Singapore. We gratefully acknowledge the support of the Canada Council for the Arts and the BC Arts Council for our publishing program.

The original art for this book was done in pencil and watercolour on Arches 140 lb cold pressed paper.

To some real-life loon seekers, Pierre, Patrick, Emily and my mother, Nancy Lloyd. Also in memory of Douglas Lloyd. — Jennifer

For D.C., who has allowed me to take over 89.3% of the studio and doesn't complain about the mess. — Kirsti

LOOKING
FOR LOONS

Written by Jennifer Lloyd

Illustrated by Kirsti Anne Wakelin

SIMPLY READ BOOKS

All was quiet in the little cottage by the lake. Slowly,
the September sunrise began to brighten the night sky.
The first morning rays streamed into the children's
room and danced on Patrick's pillow.

Patrick woke up. He slipped on his cozy housecoat and blue striped slippers. Carefully, he reached for the binoculars on the bedside table.

He crept past his sleeping sister, Emily.

"Creak," went a floorboard. Emily heard the noise. "Where are you going?" she mumbled, yawning. "To look for loons," whispered Patrick.

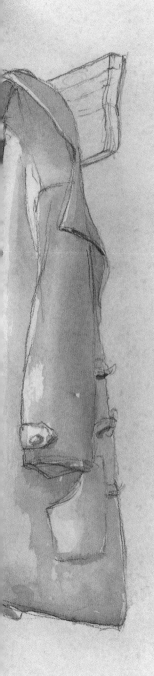

"Flip flop," went Emily's fuzzy slippers as she followed her older brother down the hallway.

Patrick gently turned the handle of the big oak door.

"Screech," went the door as it opened up onto the front porch overlooking the lake.

Grandma heard the noise. She put on her plaid dressing gown.
Tiptoeing past snoring Grandpa, she headed to the porch.

"See any loons?" asked Grandma, settling into a wooden deck
chair beside her grandchildren.

"Not yet," said Patrick.

Emily climbed onto Grandma's lap while Patrick kept a close eye
on the lake.

Just then a beaver smacked its tail on the water. Using his binoculars, Patrick watched it swim to the shore.

No loons came.

Chipmunks played in the woodpile.

No loons came.

Grandma went inside to the kitchen.

"Tweet," went the whistle of the brass kettle.

Mom heard the noise and came out onto the front porch,
carrying some old quilts. She wrapped Patrick and Emily up
in the faded blankets before sinking into an empty deck chair.

"Any luck with the loons?" she asked.

"Not yet," said Patrick.

Just then Grandma came out with a tray full of hot chocolates. Together they sipped from their steaming mugs, silently watching the misty lake.

A woodpecker tapped a red maple in the distance. Dad heard the noise and came to see his family on the porch.

Dad went into the kitchen. He poured some pancake batter into the cast iron frying pan.

"Bang," went the heavy skillet as he placed it on the stove.

Grandpa heard the noise and woke up. Wearing his red and white nightshirt and shaggy slippers, he came out onto the porch.

"Wonder where those loons could be this morning?" he said, doing his morning stretching exercises.

A cool breeze made ripples across the lake. A yellow birch leaf twirled in the air until it landed on the water.

No loons came.

A canoe glided past in the distance.

No loons came.

The smell of sizzling bacon and pancakes drifted onto the front porch. Grandpa went inside to start a fire in the stone fireplace.

Grandma went inside to pour tall glasses of orange juice.

Mom went inside to set the table and to hunt for maple syrup.

Emily's tummy started to rumble. She went inside to sit at the breakfast table.

Soon everyone was digging into Dad's delicious pancakes, all except Patrick.

Patrick stayed on the porch. He settled into his deck chair and scanned the lake one more time.

Just then a family of beautiful black and white checkered birds came into view.

"Smack," went one bird as it dove deep into the water.

"Caooooooom," went another, calling out to its family.

"Loons!" Patrick cried, jumping up from his seat.

After the last of the loons sailed past the cottage,
Patrick happily went in to join the pancake feast.